Happy Christmas to Molly, Grace and Leo,
love A & C Guillain xxx

SANTA'S WORKSHOP

First published in Great Britain 2015 by Egmont UK Limited
This edition published 2019 by Dean, an imprint of Egmont UK Limited,
The Yellow Building, 1 Nicholas Road, London, W11 4AN
www.egmont.co.uk

Text copyright © Adam and Charlotte Guillain 2015
Illustrations copyright © Lee Wildish 2015
The moral rights of the authors and illustrator have been asserted.

ISBN 978 0 6035 7579 2
70179/002
Printed in Malaysia

A CIP catalogue record for this title is available from the British Library.

Stay safe online. Egmont is not responsible for content hosted by third parties.

Egmont takes its responsibility to the planet and its inhabitants very seriously.
We aim to use papers from well-managed forests run by responsible suppliers.

# Socks for Santa

Adam & Charlotte Guillain

Lee Wildish

EGMONT

A boy called George had a magical plan,
One **Christmas Eve**, frosty and bright.
As Santa brought presents to him every year,
He'd take **gifts** to **Santa** that night.

George built a sledge and he chose Santa's gifts –
He wrapped them and packed up a box.
He dug out his backpack and put on his hat,
Then he threw in some spare **woolly socks.**

George trudged through a blizzard towards the North Pole,

But he soon didn't know where to go.

Then he spotted a **shadowy figure** ahead –
**was it Santa?**

Yes - but made of snow!

From behind the **huge snowman,**

two bears peeped at George,

Their faces were furry and white.

They suddenly scooped up big pawfuls of snow,

And called, "Time for a fun

# snowball fight!"

The polar bear cub asked George,

"Why are you here?"

"I'm looking for Santa," George said.

"I'll carry you there," said the kind mother bear,
And towards the **North Pole** they all sped.

They stopped at a workshop surrounded by trees -

Twinkly lights showed a path through the snow.

The door slowly opened and someone appeared . . .

Then a sad little elf wailed,

"Oh no!"

"What's the matter?" asked George,

with a gasp of surprise.

The elf moaned, "We're terribly late!
There's still a huge stack of **toys** to wrap up -
Santa's ready and **Christmas** can't wait!"

"We can help you!" said George, and he rolled up his sleeves,

Then he started to wrap up a toy.

The polar bears tied all the **ribbons** and **bows**.

When they'd finished, the elves danced with joy!

"Thanks!" said the elf, as he checked off his list,

"With your help we've got everything ready!"

George cheered, "Merry Christmas!" and passed around sweets,

Then he handed the bear cub a teddy!

"Come this way," said the elf,
as he opened a door,
And George dragged his box of gifts through.

FISHING TIPS

* A
* A pony
* A Star
* A Big house.
* Cuddles.
* The Moon.
* Some Milk Chocolates.
* X-Ray Vision
* A Teddy Bear.
* Fire engine
* T.V.

from...
Jimmy and Jill.

"Santa, I've brought you some presents," he called.

Then he stopped as he heard: a a a . . .

# ...choooooo!

"You're Rudolph!" said George. The deer nodded his head,

"I've got flu and my **nose has stopped glowing.**

Santa needs me to guide the sleigh later tonight,

But now I won't see where I'm going."

"Don't worry," grinned George, and he pulled out a gift,
"I've got a **torch** here you can wear!"

But then all the reindeer pulled gifts from the box -
Poor George looked round and groaned in despair.

"My presents for Santa!" cried George,
"They're all gone.
Perhaps I should pack up and go?"

He picked up his backpack and pulled on his hat,

But just then he heard . . .

# Ho ho ho!

"Santa!" gasped George, "I brought you some gifts,
But I just gave the last one away."

"That's the **spirit of Christmas!**" said Santa with joy,
"Could you help me to harness my sleigh?"

Santa grabbed his red coat and buttoned it up,
"I need to keep warm in the snow."

He sat on a stool and pulled on a sock,
But then out of a hole popped a toe!

"Now my poor foot will freeze," Santa said with a sigh.

That's when George had a brilliant idea!

He took out the last thing he had in his bag,

"You can have my **spare socks!**" he said, "Here!"

With cosy, warm feet, Santa climbed in his sleigh,
And he called out, "George, it's **Christmas Eve!**
Will you help me deliver my toys round the world?
We'll see wonders you'll never believe!"

So George jumped in the sleigh and the elves brought the sack,
And then Rudolph switched on his new light.

With a **whoosh** they were off, through the bright starry sky,
On that magical, sparkly night!